To Andrew and Hugh John
&
Jill and Susan Cotton
1942
U.M.W.

For Mum and Dad
G.T.

This is a Borzoi Book
Published by Alfred A. Knopf, Inc

Text copyright 1943, © 1990 by Ursula Moray Williams
Illustrations copyright © 1990 by Gillian Tyler
All rights reserved under International and Pan-American Copyright Conventions.
Published in the United States by Alfred A. Knopf, Inc., New York.
Distributed by Random House, Inc., New York. Originally published
in Great Britain by Julia MacRae Books, a division of
Walker Books Ltd., London, in 1990.
First American edition, 1991. Manufactured in Italy
1 2 3 4 5 6 7 8 9 10

Library of Congress Cataloging-in-Publication Data
Williams, Ursula Moray, 1911– The good little Christmas tree.
Summary: The Christmas tree of a poor peasant family
leaves their cottage on Christmas Eve and goes into the
forest in search of pretty things with which to decorate himself.
[1. Christmas trees—Fiction, 2. Christmas—Fiction]
I. Tyler, Gillian, ill. II. Title.
PZ7.W6683Gn 1990 [Fic] 90-4498
ISBN 0-679-81060-9 (trade)
ISBN 0-679-91060-3 (lib. bdg.)

The Good Little Christmas Tree

Written by

Ursula Moray Williams

Illustrated by

Gillian Tyler

ALFRED A. KNOPF

NEW YORK

O ne snowy Christmas Eve a peasant father walked home through the forest carrying a little Christmas Tree for his children.

It was neither a very tall nor a very fine tree; while the peasant, being a poor man, had no money to deck it out with gold and silver tinsel, dolls, kites, toys, and all the rest, he did not worry overmuch about it. He knew his wife would discover something in the chest to make the little tree look splendid, and his children, who had never had such a thing in the house before, would be very well pleased.

When he reached home, having tied up the little Christmas Tree in a sack, he bundled it into a corner of the kitchen behind the stove, and nothing that his boy and girl could say or do could persuade him to say a word about it.

They danced about his legs, pointing, peering, and asking a thousand curious questions while the father only shook his head; but if they approached too close to the stove to have a better look at the mysterious bundle, he  shouted out, "Take care! Take care! There is a wolf in the sack!" till they ran to hide themselves behind their mother with little shrieks of terror and excitement.

Presently they grew tired of teasing and went to bed; and when the father and mother were sure that both slept soundly, they took the Christmas Tree out of the corner and set it in a pot, where the mother hung among its branches a number of little brown cookies that she had baked, tied with scarlet thread out of the chest.

The little tree looked very proud and fine, and at first the peasant and his wife admired it with all their hearts, but little by little doubt crept in, for like all parents they wished the best for their little children; and in five minutes they were sighing and shaking their heads like two pine trees on a hill as they said to each other,

"What a pity we have not the smallest silver star nor thread of tinsel to make the branches glitter!"

"How fine a few bright candles would look among the bushy needles! How the children's eyes would sparkle to watch them flicker!"

"How dingy the branches seem! So green and bare! If we had but a few small toys and gifts for our little ones, how they would clap their hands and jump for joy!"

"However, they are good, unselfish children," the parents agreed, preparing to go to bed. "They will think the tree very pretty as it is, and make the best of it."

So off they went, sighing a little, and leaving the little Christmas Tree alone on the kitchen floor.

The tree sighed too when the peasant and his wife were gone to bed, for they were an honest pair, and he liked their kind and simple hearts. The children too were well brought up and cheerful, deserving the best that could come to them. If he could have crowded his humble branches with stars, diamonds, toys, bright ornaments, and playthings, the little Christmas Tree would have done so in a moment to please so worthy a family, and he stood

for a long while thinking deeply, with the cookies in their scarlet threads dangling from his branches like so many little brown mice.

All at once the little tree quivered. One by one he gently pulled his roots out of the pot. He was so careful that not a speck of earth fell upon the clean kitchen floor as he moved across to the door and peeped outside.

The snow lay white and deep all around. The pine trees drooped with it, but the world was well awake.

Far up in the Heavenly Meadows the baby Angels were preparing for a party.

There were wolves prowling in the forest, and a peddler, resting for the night, burned a fire to keep them away.

Mass was being sung in the far-off church, while by the

light of the moon gnomes and goblins were digging for diamonds under the snow.

Down by the stream a poor boy fished through a hole in the ice, hoping to get something for his supper, and Old Father Christmas, whom the peasants sometimes call St. Nicholas, came walking through the forest with a sack over his shoulder.

The little Christmas Tree closed the door quietly behind him and ran out into the snow, with the cookies on his branches bobbing up and down like little brown mice as he hurried along.

He ran into a clearing where the gnomes and goblins were digging for diamonds. So busy were they that scarcely one looked up to notice him.

"What will you take for a few of your diamonds?" the little Christmas Tree asked the nearest goblins.

"Ten green needles! Ten green needles!" said the goblins, who used Christmas-tree needles for threading their necklaces of precious stones.

But when the little Christmas Tree had handed over his needles and had received three diamonds in exchange, the goblins suddenly caught sight of the cookies hanging on his branches, and called out,

"Ten green needles and a round brown cookie!"

Now, the little Christmas Tree did not intend to part with any of the cookies the peasant mother had made for her children, but in order to pacify the goblins he had to give them first another ten, and then a further dozen, of his green needles, after which he left them and trotted on

his way, with the diamonds sparkling among his branches and the cookies bobbing up and down like little brown mice.

When he had left the goblins far behind, he came on a circle of scarlet toadstools, so bright and splendid with their red tops all spotted with white that he knew it would delight the children to see a few peeping from among his needles.

But he had hardly helped himself to a handful before he heard a terrible baying, which came nearer and nearer and nearer. Surrounding him was a ring of wolves, their tongues hanging out, their eyes green and hungry.

"Don't you know better than to pick scarlet toadstools?" they asked the little Christmas Tree. "Don't you know that every time you pluck one a bell rings in the Wolves' Den?"

"What will you take for your red toadstools?" the little Christmas Tree asked, trembling with fear.

"Twenty green needles! Twenty green needles!" said the wolves, who used Christmas-tree needles for picking thorns out of their paws. But when the little tree had plucked out the needles, they noticed the cookies hanging among his branches, and growled out,

"Twenty green needles and two brown cookies!"

Now, the little Christmas Tree did not intend to let the wolves have any of the cookies the peasant mother had baked for her children, so he made one bound out of the circle, shaking a shower of sharp needles into the wolves' faces, sending them howling into the forest. He then went on his way, with the toadstools gleaming, the diamonds glittering, and the cookies bobbing about like little brown mice.

Now he came to a stream in which all movement seemed frozen. But underneath the ice the fish still swam in the current, and here, beside a bridge hung with silver icicles, a poor boy had made a hole in the ice and was fishing for his supper.

The Christmas Tree was about to cross the bridge when he noticed the icicles, and thought how pretty a few would look hanging from the tips of his boughs like spears.

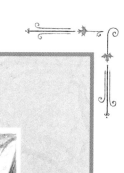

"What will you take for a few of those icicles?" he asked the fisher-boy.

"They are not mine to sell," the poor boy replied. "God made the icicles; I suppose He means us to take what we please. But pray tread carefully, or you will frighten away my little fishes."

The little Christmas Tree was so pleased with the boy's courtesy that when he had broken away a few beautiful icicles he handed some of his own green needles to the fisher-boy to make new hooks.

The boy thanked him gratefully, but his eyes strayed so wistfully toward the cookies hanging among the branches that the little tree felt much perplexed.

He could not part with any of the cookies the peasant mother had made for her children, but he said, "If you wish, you may take one bite out of my largest cookie, for I feel sure that is what any mother would wish!"

The boy eagerly did as he was told, and immediately felt as if he had risen from a banquet of roast goose, turkey, venison, plum pudding, mince pies, jellies, and dessert, while the little Christmas Tree hurried on his way, with the icicles sparkling, the toadstools gleaming, the diamonds glittering, and the cookies bobbing about like little brown mice.

Soon he met a procession of people who were wending their way through the forest to church.

All were carrying candles, which they lit as they passed through the door, where already a great number of people were singing and praising God.

The little Christmas Tree crept in behind them to listen. In the nave stood trees a great deal taller than he, their branches ablaze with colored candles that flickered

as if they too were singing anthems.

The little tree dared not ask for a candle, so he stood close by the door, listening and watching for quite a long while.

Presently an old man and a young girl came into the church. The girl took colored candles out of her basket, lighted them, and tied them on to the branches of the little Christmas Tree.

"There! That will please the good Angels and amuse some poor child on Christmas morning," said the girl.

But the old man grumbled, "Look at all those cookies hanging on the branches! They will do no good there! They will go bad! The mice will eat them during the night! They ought to be cut off and given to the poor!"

The little Christmas Tree trembled so much at the old man's words that quite a shower of green needles fell on the floor round the young girl's feet, and as she and the old man walked up the church to join the singing the little tree quickly slipped through the door and out into the forest, with the candles flickering, the icicles sparkling, the toadstools gleaming, the diamonds glittering, and the cookies bobbing about like little brown mice.

Soon he had left the church far behind.

Deep in the forest he came upon a peddler sitting by his dying fire. Beside him all his wares were spread out on the snow—puppets, boats, knives, ribbons, shawls, a fine wooden horse, and a dainty little pair of red slippers.

"What will you take for that wooden horse and that dainty pair of slippers?" asked the little Christmas Tree.

"Enough wood to make my fire blaze. I am freezing to death!" replied the peddler.

The little Christmas Tree began to throw handfuls of his green needles into the fire, but they only smoldered. Then he broke off some of his lower twigs. They crackled a little and went out. Then he broke off his best branch, and the fire burst into a bright blaze.

The peddler gave the wooden horse to the little Christmas Tree, but when he saw the cookies hanging on

the branches, a greedy look came into his eyes and he said, "If you want the slippers too, you must give me three of those round brown cookies!"

But the little Christmas Tree did not intend to part with any of the cookies the peasant mother had made for her children.

"Oh no!" said he, "that was not our bargain at all! But I will give you another branch to keep your fire alight, and you shall give me the red slippers."

The peddler grumbled and complained, but before he could change his mind the little Christmas Tree threw another branch on the fire, picked up the slippers, and ran away with them into the forest, with the wooden horse prancing, the candles flickering, the icicles sparkling, the toadstools gleaming, the diamonds glittering, and the cookies bobbing about like little brown mice.

He ran right into the Heavenly Meadows, where the baby Angels were holding their party.

They were so pleased to see him they clustered round him, caressing him with their soft little wings. Their pink toes peeped out from under their white nightgowns, and they clapped their little pink hands together in joy and delight.

When they had danced around him nearly a hundred times, they began to tie their brightest stars to his boughs. No wonder that the little Christmas Tree glowed with pleasure and gratitude!

He had very few needles left on his branches, but he offered them all as playthings to the baby Angels.

But when they grew tired of playing with the pretty green needles, they began to beg for the cookies, stretching out their little hands for them and clamoring, as children will.

Now, the little Christmas Tree did not intend to part with any of the cookies the peasant mother had made for her children, but the baby Angels had been so kind to him, and their rosy faces were so beseeching, that he had not the heart to refuse them, so at last he said: "Each of you may take a tiny bite out of just one cookie, for I feel sure that is what any mother would wish!"

But when the baby Angels had had one bite, they all wanted another, and to escape them the little Christmas Tree had to take to his heels and run until he had left the

Heavenly Meadows far behind, with the stars shining, the slippers flapping, the wooden horse prancing, the candles flickering, the icicles sparkling, the toadstools gleaming, the diamonds glittering, and the cookies bobbing about like little brown mice.

He ran till the forest was dark again, and there he found a pool, so deep and so clear that the ice had not covered it at all.

"I will have just one drink of cool water," said the little Christmas Tree, "then I must be going home."

But when he bent over the pool and saw his reflection

in the moonlight, he was so overcome by his miserable appearance that he shrank back into the snow as if he wished to hide himself completely. Gone were his bushy needles with their pale green tips, the jaunty fingers outstretched from each sturdy bough. Some of the boughs themselves were gone, leaving jagged, miserable stumps behind. It was as if the stars, the slippers, the horse, the candles, the icicles, the toadstools, and the diamonds hung on the arms of some ragged scarecrow!

He was ashamed to go home!

While the little Christmas Tree lay almost dying of shame in the snow, someone came tramping through the forest, bringing with him joy and gladness.

St. Nicholas is the children's saint. Sometimes they call him Old Father Christmas, and sometimes Santa Claus, and they credit him with all kinds of strange tricks and ways. They say he drives reindeer across the starry skies, halting them on snowy roofs to dive down chimneys with loads of gifts for stockings, sabots, and shoes. They leave presents for him, milk and cake and wine, and hay in the shoes for his reindeer. They know very little about him, but they say a great deal, and every little child loves him dearly.

Tonight the saint carried a splendid Christmas Tree over his shoulder, nearly as tall as a house, and every branch bushy with needles.

When the little Christmas Tree saw him coming through the trees, he rose up, trembling with shame, huddling his poor bare branches round him as if to make himself out to be as small as a little berry bush close by.

"Oh please, kind sir," said the little Christmas Tree. "Please grant me a favor, for pity's sake!"

When St. Nicholas stopped to listen to him, the little tree began very fast and piteously, "I beg you, kind sir, to take off my branches the shining stars, the slippers, the wooden horse, the candles, the icicles, the toadstools, the diamonds, and above all, the little cookies tied with scarlet thread, and to tie them on the branches of that splendid tree you carry! Then of your kindness will you take the tree to the cottage at the end of the forest, and leave it at the door? For I have become such a scarecrow," said the little tree, sobbing, "that I am ashamed to go home!"

But St. Nicholas smiled very kindly at the little Christmas Tree, stroking him with his hand on his poor, bare branches.

At the first touch the tree prickled all over! At the second he had the strangest sensation, as if each twig were bursting and popping open like so many buttons!

His needles were growing again!

As they grew thicker and thicker, new boughs sprang from the torn stumps till, reflected in the forest pool, he

now saw a splendid tree, among whose branches shone bright stars and dangled silver icicles.

The candles, slippers, horse, toadstools, diamonds, and cookies were almost hidden behind the wealth of fresh green that covered the tree from top to toe.

"We will go home together!" said Old Father Christmas.

As they walked through the quiet forest they passed the
Heavenly Meadows, and all the baby Angels fell in
procession behind them. The peddler left his glowing fire

and followed behind the Angels. The people were leaving church. They joined the peddler, still singing their Christmas hymns. The boy at the frozen stream picked up his basket of silver fish to follow the crowd, while the wolves skulked out of the trees, mild as lambs, trotting with the rest.

The gnomes and goblins put down their picks and shovels to follow the wolves, while in front of them all walked St. Nicholas and the little Christmas Tree, with the stars twinkling, the slippers dancing, the wooden horse galloping, the candles flaming, the icicles dazzling, the toadstools shining, the diamonds flashing, and the cookies bobbing about like little brown mice, each with a tiny bite taken out of it, except the largest, which had two!

The peasant's children were awake and peeping through the window, as children will on Christmas night.

"Look! Look what is coming through the forest! Look at the wolves! Look at the gnomes and goblins! Look at the sweet little Angels in their white nightgowns! Look at the people singing, and the poor boy carrying his basket of fish! Look at the peddlerman! And *look*!…There is Old Father Christmas, and he is bringing us a little Christmas Tree all covered with…Oh! Quick! Quick! Get back into bed and pull the bedclothes over our heads as quick as we can, or we shall never get anything at all!"